For Seb and Hamish

JANETTA OTTER-BARRY BOOKS

First published in Great Britain and in the USA in 2014 by
Frances Lincoln Children's Books, 74–77 White Lion Street, London N1 4PF
www.franceslincoln.com

This edition published in Great Britain and in the USA in 2014

A catalogue record for this book is available from the British Library.

ISBN 978-1-84780-412-9

Set in KosmikPlainOne

Printed in China

1 3 5 7 9 8 6 4 2

Seb and Hamish

Written by Jude Daly
Illustrated by Niki Daly

FRANCES LINCOLN
CHILDREN'S BOOKS

Seb and Mama were going visit
their new neighbour, Mrs Kenny.
Seb was looking very smart in his tiger top.
Mama was looking very smart too.

Mama lifted Seb up to ring the bell.

Inside, Mrs Kenny was busy putting
smiley faces on some cookies.
Seb rang the bell again.

Ding-dong, ding-dong!

Hamish rushed to the door.
Woof!
Woof!
Woof!
Woof!

Seb covered his ears
and hid behind Mama.

He grabbed Mama's hand and pulled her away from the door. Then in a tiny little voice he said,

"Home."

Mrs Kenny opened the front door.
She was smiling, and holding
Hamish in her arms.
"Hello, Tiger," said Mrs Kenny.
"Woof!" went Hamish.
"Up," said Seb in his tiny voice.

Mama picked Seb up.
"Hamish is just saying hello," she said.
Seb's lip trembled.
He shrank into his top
like a tortoise into its shell.

Woof-woof,
woof-woof!

"Oh, dearie me," said Mrs Kenny.
"He's just SO excited to meet you."

Woof-woof, woof-woof!

"Home," whispered Seb.

Mrs Kenny put Hamish into her bedroom and closed the door. Seb checked the door to make sure it was properly shut.

In the kitchen, Seb saw
Mrs Kenny's toys and forgot
all about Hamish.
He wrapped his blankey around
a teddy and put it in the train
with his juice and some
smiley faces.

Clickety-clack, clickety-clack!

The train went through Mama's legs,
under the table and round Mrs Kenny's chair.

It went down the passage.

Clickety-clack, Clickety-clack...

Then it stopped for a tea break.

PUNCH
&
JUDY
strawberry
5

While Seb was eating a smiley face,
the nose fell off and disappeared
under Mrs Kenny's bedroom door.

Seb poked his finger under the door.
Something gave it a soft lick.

And when Seb looked through
the gap, two bright eyes
looked back at him.

"Hello," said Seb.

Sniff-sniff, sniff-sniff.

"Hello, Hamish," said Seb.

Sniff-sniff, sniff-sniff.

Ever so slowly, Seb opened the door
and peeped through. Hamish's tail
was wagging so much it made his
bottom wiggle-waggle.
"Funny Hamish," said Seb.

Seb touched Hamish's smooth silky head. He felt a floppy ear. He stroked it and he stroked it.

It was even softer than his blankey.

Mama and Mrs Kenny had been chattering away like
two busy birds when Mrs Kenny said,
"Time to check up on the train driver!"

So Mama and Mrs Kenny tiptoed down the passage . . .

and there they found Seb.

He was fast asleep –

with his new best friend.